Journey
ATHENS

USA

Table of Contents

©2004 by GRIFFIN PUBLISHING GROUP/UNITED STATES OLYMPIC COMMITTEE

Published by Griffin Publishing Group under license from the United States Olympic Committee. The use of Olympic-related marks and terminology is authorized by the United States Olympic Committee pursuant to Title *36 U.S. Code* Section 220506. U.S. Olympic Committee, One Olympic Plaza, Colorado Springs, CO 80909.

10 9 8 7 6 5 4 3 2 1

ISBN   1-58000-121-1

TCM   3748

DIRECTOR OF OPERATIONS . . . . Robin L. Howland
PROJECT MANAGER . . . . Bryan K. Howland
AUTHOR . . . . Cynthia Holzschuher, M.Ed.
EDITOR . . . . Ellyn Siskind, M.A.
COVER DESIGNER . . . . Brenda DiAntonis
ART MANAGER . . . . Kevin Barnes
ART DIRECTOR . . . . CJae Froshay
ILLUSTRATOR . . . . Ken Tunell

Griffin Publishing Group
18022 Cowan, Suite 202
Irvine, CA 92614
www.griffinpublishing.com

Manufactured in the United States of America

Published in association with
and distributed by:
Teacher Created Materials, Inc.
6421 Industry Way
Westminster, CA 92683
www.teachercreated.com

Welcome to Athens, Greece

Athens, the capital of Greece, is home to about five million people. Its location on the Mediterranean Sea has made Athens an important harbor which supports the country's shipping and fishing industries. It is the industrial, political, and cultural center of Greece.

Athens was the birthplace of the ancient Olympic Games and host to the first modern Games in 1896. Now, more than one hundred years later, the city has prepared for the arrival of hundreds of thousands of visitors from around the world. Plans have been made to assure their safety and comfort.

An international airport, two underground railway systems, and hundreds of miles of new roads will make traveling easy. Visitors will stay in private homes or refurbished hotels. The new Olympic Village will house athletes and the historic Panathinaikon Stadium has been restored for the opening and closing ceremonies.

Thinking about the Olympic Games:

* What kinds of businesses will profit from the Athens Olympic Games?

   _____

   _____

* In what ways will the residents of Athens benefit from the Olympic Games?

   _____

   _____

* How will hosting the Olympic Games affect daily life for the residents of Athens?

   _____

   _____

* Explain how and why hosting the Olympic Games can be good for a city.

   _____

   _____

Research: Why do you think that Athens has been an Olympic host more often than any other city? Use the following search words to view photos or read more about the topic: *Athens, Attica, Greece, Olympia, Olympic Games*

_____

_____

_____

_____

_____

_____

 # Athens Traveler

Besides watching the Olympic Games, visitors will want to spend some time getting to know more about the host city. Pretend you own a travel agency and want to organize a tour of Athens and the surrounding area. You will need to create a brochure describing the historical and cultural attractions available for your clients.

Use the Internet to help you with this project. Look for city maps, photos, and hotel information to add to your brochure. Here are some search words: *Athens, Greece, Attica, Athena, Acropolis, Parthenon, Greek National Tourism Organization.*

Fold a paper in thirds as illustrated below to make the brochure. Add illustrations to make it more attractive. Be sure to include the following information:

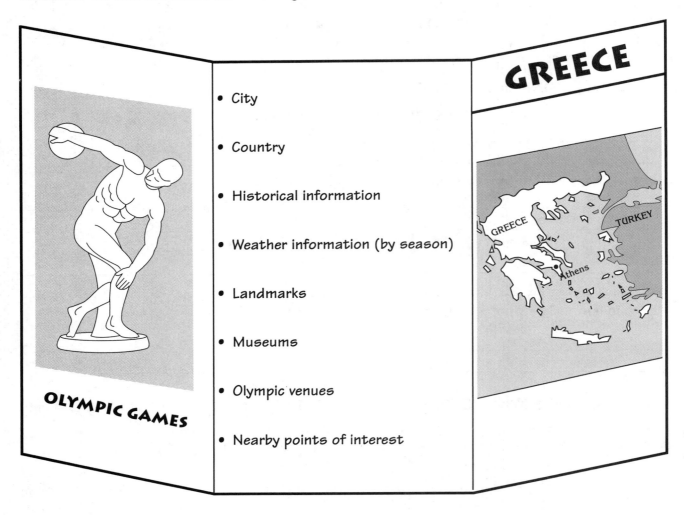

OLYMPIC GAMES

- City
- Country
- Historical information
- Weather information (by season)
- Landmarks
- Museums
- Olympic venues
- Nearby points of interest

GREECE

Extension: Bring a variety of travel brochures to the class for the students to examine. After reviewing them, take a class vote on which destination is the most appealing. Why? What do the students think are the most important factors when selecting a vacation location? Would their parents agree?

Getting There Is Fun!

Athletes and visitors from around the world will be traveling to Athens for the Olympic Games. They will be arranging transportation for themselves and their families. What types of transportation do you think you would use to get from the city where you live to the Athens 2004 Olympic Games?

_____

_____

Complete this activity using the map your teacher will give you.*

1. Locate your state and mark the city where you live on the map.

2. Locate Athens, Greece.

3. Use a ruler to draw a straight line between your city and Athens.

4. Label all states, countries, and bodies of water that your line passes through.

5. List them below:

States	Countries	Bodies of Water
_____	_____	_____
_____	_____	_____
_____	_____	_____
_____	_____	_____
_____	_____	_____

*To the teacher:** If you live east of the Mississippi River, use Map A; if you live west of the Mississippi River, use Map B.

Extensions:

• You have investigated the shortest way to reach Athens from your home in the exercise above. Working with a partner, complete a similar activity traveling in the opposite direction around the world.

• What would be the least expensive way for you to travel to Athens from your city? Research different modes of transportation and their costs. How long would each mode take?

Getting There Is Fun! *(cont.)*

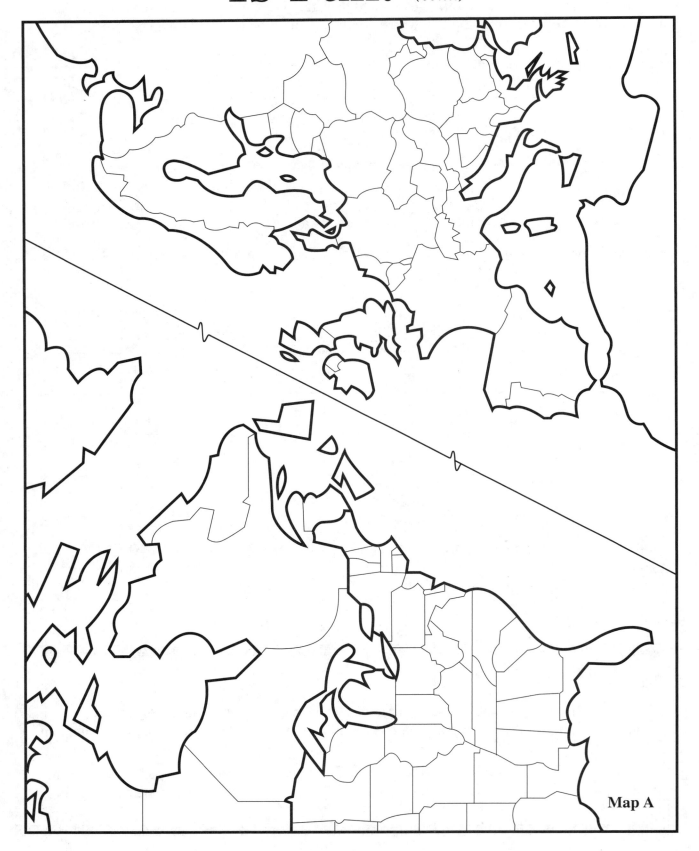

Map A

Getting There
Is Fun! *(cont.)*

Map B

Acropolis Hill

The **Acropolis** is the most famous landmark in the city of Athens. The Greeks built the Acropolis on a hill called the "Sacred Rock" and used it as a religious center and military fortress. From the top of the hill, visitors can see a beautiful view of Athens and the Saronic Gulf.

There are ruins of three temples at the Acropolis. Visitors enter the temple area through the **Propylaea**, a large gateway. The three temples, **The Parthenon, The Temple of Athena Nike,** and **The Erechtheion** were all built between 450–30 B.C.

The largest and most famous building, The Parthenon, is made entirely of marble except for its wooden roof. One of the rooms held a large golden statue of the goddess Athena. There are paintings showing battles of the Trojan War and scenes from Greek mythology on the Parthenon's outer walls. The Parthenon is the international symbol of Greece.

There are two ancient theaters and some government buildings at the bottom of the Acropolis Hill as well as ruins of the Angora, a marketplace that served the city center.

Most artifacts from the Acropolis ruins have been stored in a nearby museum.

Answer the following questions:

What landmarks do you think Olympic athletes would most want to see in Athens?

_____

_____

How would an Athens resident explain the importance of the Acropolis Hill to a visiting athlete?

_____

_____

Use these search words to view photos or read more about the topic: *Acropolis Hill, Parthenon, Greek landmarks, Athens, Sacred Rock, Athena, Trojan War, Greek mythology*

Ancient Olympic Games

The first recorded Olympic Games, in 776 B.C., were held in the city of Olympia, Greece. The games took place in late June or early July and only athletes of pure Greek blood were allowed to take part. Winners of the ancient games brought special honor to their home towns. Often songs and poems were written about their achievements and marble statues were sculpted to show their physical strength. Few of those statues remain today, but here are some of the athletes' stories.

 Milo of Kroton was a wrestler who won six Olympic competitions. He was known to have very strong wrists and hands. It is said that when he held out his right hand with thumb pointed upwards and fingers spread no one could bend his fingers. Milo was also a brave warrior. When a neighboring town attacked Kroton, Milo entered the battle wearing his Olympic crowns and carrying only a club. He led his fellow citizens to victory.

 The boxer **Diagoras of Rhodes** was said to have had super human athletic ability. He was known to be a fair fighter. Diagoras was the winner of one Olympic boxing title. He lived long enough to see his two sons, **Damagetos** and **Akousilaos**, win Olympic titles in pankration and boxing. A third son, **Dorieus**, won three Olympic titles in pankration.

 Polydamas of Skotoussa was a pankratist with only one Olympic victory. The sport, a combination of wrestling and boxing, required great strength. It is said that Polydamas once stopped a fast moving, four-horse chariot and kept it from going forward. King Dareius, of Persia, heard of his strength and challenged Polydamas to fight the three best fighters in his kingdom. Even at three against one, Polydamas was the winner.

 Boxer **Melankomas of Caria** was known for his handsome body and good looks. His boxing style was to defend himself from the blows of his opponents without ever hitting them. Eventually, the other boxer grew tired and frustrated and gave up. Melankomas was praised for his strength and endurance because he could fight in the hot sun for an entire day without giving up. He exercised more than most other athletes of the time. It is said that he once held his arms up for two days without ever putting them down or resting.

Research: Use the Internet to learn more about current Greek Olympic athletes. Create a list of ten men and/or women and indicate their sport. Use these search words to help you: *2004 Greek Olympic athletes.*

 # The First Modern Olympic Games

The founder of the modern Olympic Games and Olympic Movement was a Frenchman, **Pierre de Coubertin**. He believed that exercise and sports were good for young people. In addition, Coubertin knew that Olympic athletes would make friends with people from other countries. In this way, he hoped the Olympic Games would promote understanding and world peace.

The first modern Olympic Games were held in Panathenian Stadium in Athens, Greece in 1896. Giorgios Averoff, a wealthy Greek, financed the restoration of the 50,000 seat stadium which had been built in 330 B.C. The Games began on March 25, and lasted for ten days. Here is a list of each day's events.

The Olympic Calendar 1896		**Day One** 100 meter race, the hop, step and jump, the 800 meter race, throwing the discus, the 400 meter race
Day Two fencing contest, the 110 meter race with hurdles, the long jump, the final of the 400 meters, putting the weight, weightlifting, the 1500 meter race	**Day Three** shooting, lawn tennis, cycle race	**Day Four** shooting, lawn tennis, fencing contests, the 800 meter race, parallel bars (teams), horizontal bars (teams), vaulting horse, the pommel horse, rings, horizontal bars
Day Five parallel bars (individual), climbing the rope, shooting, finals of the 100 meter race, high jump, 110 meter hurdle race, pole vault, marathon, wrestling	**Day Six** shooting, swimming, cycling, lawn tennis finals	**Day Seven** shooting finals, marathon cycle race, the torch procession and the winners banquet at the palace
Day Eight boat races, cycle races	**Day Nine** all events were canceled due to heavy rain	**Day Ten** Closing Ceremonies, when athletes were given an Olympic Games Certificate, a wild olive branch, and their medals by the King of Greece

Project: Choose one day to illustrate and explain in detail. You may create a diorama, poster, or book detailing the day's events. If you prefer, you may use all the information to create a time line showing the order of events for the 1896 Olympic Games.

 # Host Cities List

Year	Olympic Games	Winter Olympic Games
1896	Athens, Greece	**
1900	Paris, France*	**
1904	St. Louis, Missouri, USA	**
1908	London, England (Great Britain)	**
1912	Stockholm, Sweden	**
1916	Not held due to World War I	**
1920	Antwerp, Belgium	**
1924	Paris, France	Chamonix, France
1928	Amsterdam, the Netherlands	St. Moritz, Switzerland
1932	Los Angeles, California, USA	Lake Placid, New York, USA
1936	Berlin, Germany	Garmisch-Partenkirchem, Germany
1940	Not held due to World War II	Not held due to World War II
1944	Not held due to World War II	Not held due to World War II
1948	London, England (Great Britain)	St. Moritz, Switzerland
1952	Helinski, Finland	Oslo, Norway
1956	Melbourne, Australia	Cortina, Italy
1960	Rome, Italy	Squaw Valley, California, USA
1964	Tokyo, Japan	Innsbruck, Austria
1968	Mexico City, Mexico	Grenoble, France
1972	Munich, West Germany	Sapporo, Japan
1976	Montreal, Canada	Innsbruck, Austria
1980	Moscow, Russia	Lake Placid, New York, USA
1984	Los Angeles, California, USA	Sarajevo, Yugoslavia
1988	Seoul, South Korea	Calgary, Canada
1992	Barcelona, Spain	Albertville, France
1996	Atlanta, Georgia, USA	Lillehammer, Norway (1994)
2000	Sydney, Australia	Nagano, Japan (1998)
2004	Athens, Greece	Salt Lake City, Utah, USA (2002)
2008	Beijing, China	Torino, Italy (2006)

*First time women competed in the modern Olympics; they played lawn tennis.

**Winter Olympic Games began in 1924.

Opening and Closing Ceremonies

The opening ceremony for the 1896 Olympic Games was held in the Panathinaikon Stadium. Seventy thousand spectators, including members of the Greek Royal Family, listened as King George declared the Games officially open. The Greek National Hymn was played and the Crown Prince was honored as the president of the Olympic Committee.

The opening and closing ceremonies for the Athens 2004 Olympic Games will be held in the same historic stadium. It has been restored and is ready to host a spectacular performance of traditional Greek music and dance. Local citizens volunteer to perform together to welcome the world to their city.

The parade of athletes is a highlight of the opening ceremony. Greek athletes have the honor of entering the stadium first. They are followed in alphabetical order, by athletes from the other participating countries. Each group carries its national flag.

Following the parade, a representative of the host nation welcomes the athletes and declares the Games officially open. The athletes recite the Olympic oath and a flock of doves is released as a symbol of peace. The Olympic flame is lit and the ceremony usually ends with a fireworks display.

When the sixteen-day competition is over, athletes gather again in the same stadium to say goodbye to their friends, congratulate those who have won medals, and thank the spectators. This time they walk side by side with athletes from other countries. People representing the host country will make speeches telling their thoughts about the Games. The flag of the next Olympic host country is raised and people from that country invite the world to attend those Games. Finally, the Games are declared officially closed, the flame is put out, and the Olympic flag is lowered. There is usually entertainment and a fireworks display to close the ceremony.

Activities:

- **Choose a country** participating in the Games. Draw the flag of that country on large paper. Work with class members to display the flags in the school hallway. As the Games proceed, keep a tally of each country's medal winners under its flag.

- **Design a uniform** or warm up suit for an athlete from the country of your choice. The color and design should reflect that country in some way and the outfit should be suitable for wearing to the opening ceremony.

- **Write a short speech** that could be read by a representative of the host country at the opening or closing ceremony. Include a welcome or thank you to all competitors and express your hope for friendship, cooperation, and understanding among the people of the world.

- **Research** traditional forms of Greek costumes, music, and dance that might be part of the 2004 opening ceremony. Use these search terms to find information: *Greek music, Greek dance, Greek costume, Hellenic.*

Olympic Spirit

Baron Pierre de Coubertin knew that the Olympic Games would bring together athletes from around the world. He wanted the games to promote friendship, cooperation, respect, and understanding among people of different cultures. He believed that world peace would come when individuals learned to work and play together. This is the spirit of "Olympism".

Do you agree with Pierre de Coubertin's idea of Olympism? Explain.

_____

_____

List three Olympic experiences that might cause competing athletes to become friends.

1. _____

2. _____

3. _____

Think about how you can promote respect, cooperation, and friendship among your classmates and answer the following questions.

Do you have a peaceful classroom? Why? Why not?

_____

_____

_____

What can you do to help make a classroom more peaceful?

_____

_____

_____

Olympic Biography

Pierre de Coubertin was born in Paris, France, in 1863. His father was an artist and his mother was a musician. He did well in school and grew to believe that education was the key to a good future. By the age of 24, Coubertin had decided to improve the old-fashioned school system in France.

In addition to his interest in education, Coubertin was an active sportsman who enjoyed boxing, fencing, horse riding, and rowing. He knew that sports could improve the physical, intellectual, and spiritual growth of athletes. Because of this, he decided to revive the Olympic Games.

Coubertin wanted to encourage and reward talented athletes, but he also hoped to give people from different countries a chance to meet and become friends. In this spirit, he founded the International Olympic Committee (IOC) on June 23, 1894, and established its headquarters in Lausanne, Switzerland. Two years later, in 1896, the first Olympic Games of the modern era were held in Athens, Greece. Coubertin continued to believe in the spirit of the Olympic Games until his death from a heart attack on September 2, 1937.

Answer the following questions:

1. Where was Pierre de Coubertin born?_____

2. What sports did he enjoy? _____

3. In what year did he found the IOC? _____

4. Where is the IOC headquarters located? _____

5. What was the cause of Coubertin's death? _____

6. Why did Coubertin want to revive the Olympic Games? _____

7. How old was Pierre de Coubertin when he died? (**Hint:** Subtract the year he was born from the year he died.) _____

   _____

   _____

8. Do you think the Olympic Games lead to friendship and understanding in the world? Explain.

   _____

   _____

   _____

Olympic Motto

Use the words in the circles to answer the clues. Cross out each answer as you use it. The words that are left will complete the bonus sentence.

1. Ran the first marathon
2. Founder of the 1896 Olympic Games
3. Capital city of Greece
4. Donated money to restore stadium in 1896
5. Most dangerous sport in ancient games
6. Ancient games winner's prize
7. Wrestler in ancient games

8. Stadium restored for 2004 Games
9. Decathlon number
10. Second place medal
11. Five Olympic flag symbols
12. Lit by the sun
13. Triathlon number

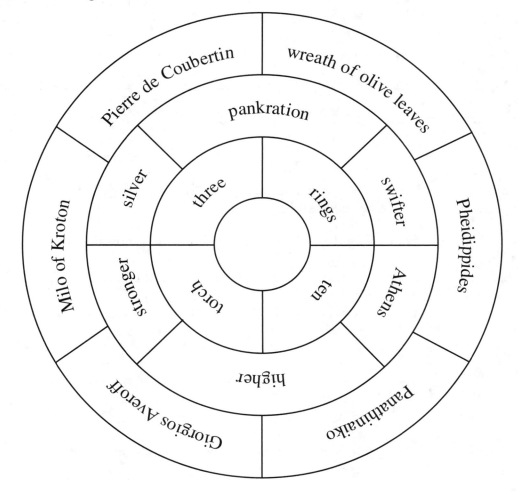

Bonus: The Olympic motto is "_____, _____, _____."

To the Teacher: Fold back this answer section before making copies.

Answers: 1) Pheidippides   2) Pierre de Coubertin   3) Athens   4) Giorgios Averoff
5) pankration   6) wreath of olive leaves   7) Milo of Kroton   8) Panathinaiko   9) ten
10) silver   11) rings   12) torch   13) three

Bonus Question: The Olympic motto is "Swifter, higher, stronger".

 # Do Your Best

This is the Olympic athlete's creed:

"The most important thing in the Olympic Games is not to win, but to take part, just as the most important thing in life is not the triumph but the struggle. The essential thing is not to have conquered but to have fought well."

Explain the meaning of the Olympic Creed in your own words.

_____

_____

_____

_____

This creed is a good lesson for life. You can be proud of yourself if you work hard and do your best. You do not always need to win to be successful.

Make a list of five things you do every day. Explain how you can be successful.

1. _____

2. _____

3. _____

4. _____

5. _____

How will working hard and doing your best every day prepare you to be an adult?

_____

_____

_____

_____

Competition

Some people play sports for fun and exercise. Others perform best when they are testing themselves against a record speed, distance, or rival athlete. They enjoy working for awards or medals. These competitors often do well in many areas of life, not just athletics.

While the Olympic Games stress participation and sportsmanship, medal winners have always been honored by their countrymen. In ancient times, they may have been given free food and lodging. Modern winners are pictured on cereal boxes and may be well paid for endorsements.

I. Sports Competitions

What is your favorite indoor or outdoor sport? Why? _____

_____

How do you feel when you win? When you lose?_____

_____

_____

II. Non–Sport Competitions

What other kinds of competitions have you been part of? _____

_____

Did you enjoy the experience? Explain._____

_____

III. All Competitions

Think of ways in which all competitions are alike. _____

_____

Transfer this information to a Venn diagram, comparing your favorite competitive activity with all competitive activities. Show the ways in which they are alike, and the ways in which they are different. Name the diagram and label the sections.

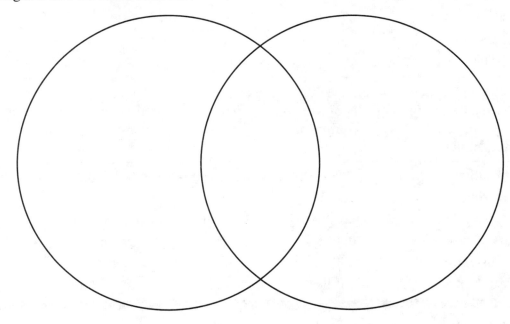

Greek Medal Winners

Wrestling is the oldest sport in the Olympic Games. Wrestlers are divided into groups based on their body weight. There are two styles of wrestling: Greco-Roman and freestyle. In the Greco-Roman style, a wrestler may not hold his opponent below the waist or grip his legs. In freestyle, wrestlers may use their legs to grab, lift, and control an opponent. A wrestler wins by pinning his opponent or by a technical fall.

These Greek athletes have recently won Olympic medals in **wrestling**:

Krastanov, Alexandros	freestyle	bronze	Sydney	2000
Holides, Haralambos	Greco-Roman	bronze	Los Angeles	1984
			Seoul	1988
Thanopoulos, Dimitrios	Greco-Roman	silver	Los Angeles	1984

Athletes competed by lifting heavy stones in the ancient Olympics. There are two basic lifts: the snatch and the clean-and-jerk. In the snatch, the lifter pulls up on the barbell, squats under it, stands and raises the barbell overhead with straight arms in one move. In the clean-and-jerk, the lifter raises the bar chest high (the clean), then overhead from a split leg position (the jerk). The winner is the athlete who lifts the greatest amount of weight in both lifts combined.

These Greek athletes have recently won Olympic medals in **weightlifting**:

Kokkas, Leonidas	silver	Atlanta	1996
Leonides, Valerios	silver	Atlanta	1996
Mitrou, Viktor	silver	Sydney	2000
Sabanis, Leonidas	silver	Atlanta	1996
		Sydney	2000
Dimas, Pyrros	gold	Barcelona	1992
		Atlanta	1996
		Sydney	2000
Kahniashvili, Kakhi	gold	Barcelona	1992
		Atlanta	1996
		Sydney	2000
Hatzijoannou, Ioanna	bronze	Sydney	2000

The sprint was the only track and field event in the ancient Olympic Games. Since those early Games, several other events requiring the skills of running, jumping, and throwing have become popular. Each of these sports has specific rules and equipment. Winners are among the fastest, strongest, and most accurate Olympic athletes.

These Greek athletes have recently won Olympic medals in **track and field**:

Thanou, Katerina	100m	silver	Sydney	2000
Manjani, Mirella	javelin	silver	Sydney	2000
Kelesidou, Anastasia	discus	silver	Sydney	2000
Kenteris, Konstantinos	200m	gold	Sydney	2000
Patoulidou, Paraskevi	hurdles	gold	Barcelona	1992

Greek Medal Winners *(cont.)*

Use the information on the previous page to create a bar graph showing the number of medals won by Greek athletes in Barcelona, Atlanta, and Sydney in **wrestling, weightlifting**, and **track and field**. Fill in the medal winners at the Athens 2004 Olympic Games as well, if the information is available.

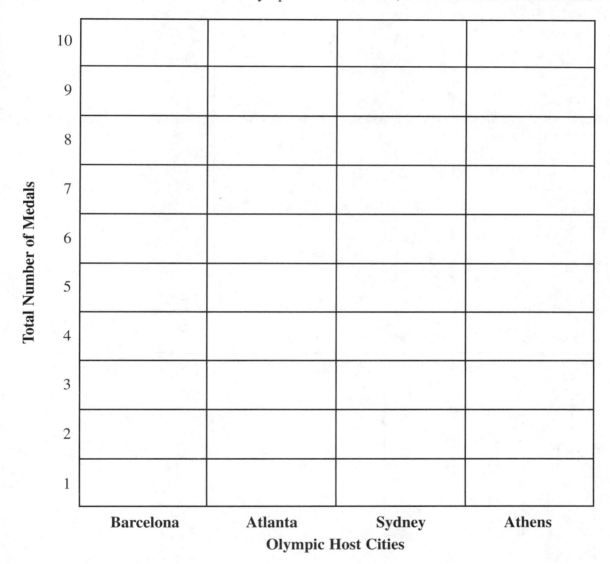

Total Number of Medals (y-axis: 1, 2, 3, 4, 5, 6, 7, 8, 9, 10)

Barcelona   Atlanta   Sydney   Athens

Olympic Host Cities

Extension:

- Use reference books or the Internet to find additional information about other athletic achievements of one of these Greek athletes. Write a brief report to tell what you've learned.

- Use reference books or the Internet to find out which medals the following Greek Olympic athletes won: Melissanides Loannis, Mouroutsos Mihalis, and Tambakos Demosothenis. When did they win their medals, and in which sport?

 # Trading Cards

Use this form to make a trading card for a Greek athlete or your favorite Olympic athlete. Draw his/her picture (or use one from the Internet or a news or magazine article), then add important facts to complete the form. Cut out the shape, fold it in half, and glue the front to the back.

Athlete:

Sport:

Country:

Medals:

Important Facts

Fair Play

All Olympic athletes make a promise to play fair. Here are the words of their oath:

"In the name of all competitors, I promise that we shall take part in these Olympic Games, respecting and abiding by the rules which govern them, in the true spirit of sportsmanship, for the glory of the sport, and the honor of our teams."

Fair competition is the Olympic ideal. Athletes must follow the rules of their sport and treat each other with respect. In this way, Olympic athletes honor their sport.

1. How would you explain the Olympic ideal of sportsmanship to a young athlete?

   _____

   _____

   _____

2. Is it important for all players to follow the rules of a sport? Why? Why not?

   _____

   _____

   _____

3. List three things an Olympic athlete might do to dishonor his or her sport.

   _____

   _____

   _____

Olympic Oath

All Olympic athletes make a promise at the opening ceremony of the Games that expresses their commitment to fair competition. To solve the puzzle and answer the question, begin at START. Follow the arrows to move around the circle, writing every other letter in the blanks (starting with **B**). When you have completed one time around the circle, reverse the direction (starting with **R**) and continue writing every other letter until you finish the phrase.

What does an Olympic athlete promise to do?

__ __ __ __ __ __ __ __ __ __ __ __ and __ __ __ __ __ __ __ __ __ __ __

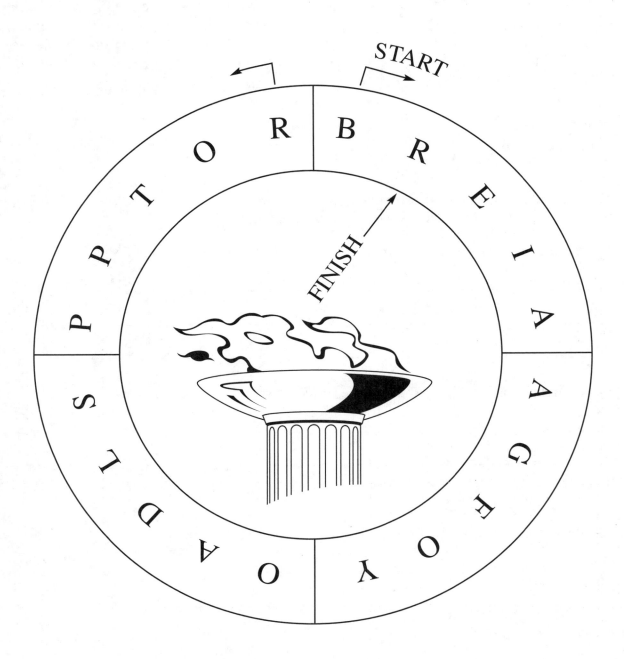

22

Identify the Sport

Read the clues and name the sport. Use the Word Bank to help you.

1. Competitors jump from a springboard or a platform.

   _____

2. The middle ring of the target is worth ten points.

   _____

3. The playing field is called a diamond.

   _____

4. Field goals count as two points and free throws as one.

   _____

5. A team of 6 - 8 riders is called a **peloton** in this road race.

   _____

6. Dressage riders must perform 32 different movements.

   _____

7. Men compete in six events, including the pommel horse and still rings.

   _____

8. If the birdie hits the ground, the point is over.

   _____

9. This game was first called Ping-Pong because of the sound made by the ball hitting the paddle.

   _____

10. In this water sport, the individual or crew with the fewest points is the winner.

    _____

11. Players may hit the ball only with their head, chest, thighs, or feet.

    _____

12. Races are held in long course pools with 6–10 lanes.

    _____

Word Bank

diving	table tennis	cycling	badminton
baseball	sailing	equestrian	swimming
basketball	soccer	gymnastics	archery

To the Teacher: Fold back this answer section before making copies.

Answers: 1) diving 2) archery 3) baseball 4) basketball 5) cycling 6) equestrian
7) gymnastics 8) badminton 9) table tennis 10) sailing 11) soccer 12) swimming

 # Olympic Village

The Athens **Olympic Village** will host 16,000 athletes and team officials during the 2004 Olympic Games. The village has two main sections: **The Residential Zone,** which has 2,292 apartments for the athletes and **The International Zone,** which includes the main entrance, shopping centers, an Olympic museum, and other administration buildings. The Olympic Village is the largest housing project ever built in Greece.

The athletes' comfort and convenience in the village are most important. Some rooms have been specially designed for taller athletes. The apartments will be private and quiet, well separated from banks, shops, medical centers, places of worship, entertainment, and dining halls which are open twenty–four hours a day. All athletes will have easy access to transportation to each of the sports venues.

Security is always a concern at the Olympic Village because athletes must feel safe in order to compete well. The staff wants the athletes to feel at home while they are living in the village. In order to provide excellent service, employees must be able to speak several languages.

Complete one of these assignments:

1. Design an Olympic Village using the information in the article above.

2. Pretend you are in charge of security at the village. Explain what you would do to insure the safety of the athletes.

3. Choose two jobs in the village. Which job would be best/worst? Explain your choice.

4. Make a list of characteristics you would look for if you were in charge of hiring Olympic Village staff. Write five questions you would ask at an interview.

5. Choose your favorite summer Olympic sport. Make a list of items you would need to take if you were an athlete packing for the Games.

6. Sketch an exhibit that might be displayed in the Olympic Museum.

7. How might the Olympic Village be used after the Games are over? Explain your idea and give five supporting reasons.

8. Imagine you are an athlete living in the village. Write a schedule telling what you will do on a day when you are not competing.

Training Table

It is expected that six thousand meals will be served every hour at the Athens Olympic Village! Workers will plan and prepare special meals for athletes using the same recipes and foods they would eat in their home countries. All athletes need good nutrition so they will have the strength and energy to do their best.

Choose a country and research its traditional foods. On the plate, draw a meal with foods from at least four different food groups that might be chosen by an athlete from that country. Use the writing lines to list the foods and indicate their food groups.

Country: _____

_____

_____

_____

_____

Bonus: Athletes from different sports might require different amounts or types of foods to do their best. Choose two different sports and explain why the athletes might need or want different or additional foods.

 # Olympic Appeal

Pretend you are an advertising executive for a large producer of packaged foods. You have been asked to design a line of snack-sized health foods that could be sold from vending machines in the Olympic Village. You may work alone or in teams of three to come up with ideas for three different foods. Complete one form for each product.

Product Name: _____

Product Description (package contents): _____

_____

Slogan: _____

Package Description: _____

_____

Cost: _____

Why do you think Olympic athletes will want to eat this product? _____

_____

_____

Illustrate the package.

Souvenir Store

Official Olympic Games merchandise is only produced and distributed by licensed companies that have been approved by the Athens 2004 Organizing Committee. All the items were selected because they are of good quality and can be used by people around the world who support the Olympic Games. There are many stores in Athens that sell licensed products—two are at the airport, others are in the center of the city or near Olympic venues.

Look at the products for sale in this souvenir shop. On another paper, write five word problems using addition, subtraction, or multiplication explaining what you or those traveling with you would like to buy. Trade papers with a friend and solve the problems.

 # Track and Field Jeopardy

Answer each clue by writing a question. Use the word bank to help you.

Example: Foot races are run on this.

　　　　<u>What is a track?</u>

1. This Greek runner won the 1896 Olympic marathon.

　　• Who is _____?

2. This sport was used in prehistoric times for hunting.

　　• What is the _____?

3. In this sport the athlete tries to jump as far as possible.

　　• What is the _____?

4. In this sport the athlete tries to throw a solid metal ball as far as possible.

　　• What is the _____?

5. Four team members pass a baton in these races.

　　• What are _____?

6. All athletic events include these skills.

　　• What are _____?

7. In this sport the athlete tries to throw a flat, wood or metal circle as far as possible.

　　• What is the _____?

8. Athletes must jump over ten barriers in these short runs.

　　• What are _____?

9. This venue will host the track and field events in the Athens 2004 games.

　　• What is _____?

10. The decathlon is a two-day contest with this number of events.

　　• What is _____?

Word Bank

Spyridon Louis	running, jumping, and throwing
discus throw	hurdles
long jump	javelin throw
shotput	The Athens Olympic Sports Complex
relays	ten

Diving

In the Olympic Games, seven judges give each diver a score from 0–10. The **highest and lowest scores are thrown out** and **the remaining scores are added.** Then, this **total is multiplied by 0.6**. To get the diver's final score, that **total is multiplied by a number given each dive** based on its degree of difficulty. The degree of difficulty can range from 1.1–3.0.

Based on the information given above, list the four steps you must take to determine an athlete's final score:

- Step 1: _____
- Step 2: _____
- Step 3: _____
- Step 4: _____

Now, look at the scores below. Assume that all the divers did a 2.8 dive. Use a separate sheet of paper to compute final totals. Which athletes won the gold, silver, and bronze medals?

Judges	1	2	3	4	5	6	7	Final Score
Men								_____
Tom	9.1	8.9	9.0	8.8	9.2	9.0	9.1	_____
Bob	9.4	8.8	9.1	9.2	9.4	8.9	9.0	_____
Joe	8.9	9.4	9.2	9.0	8.8	9.5	9.0	_____
Paul	9.3	9.0	8.9	8.9	9.1	9.0	9.2	_____
Tony	9.1	9.1	9.2	9.4	8.8	9.0	8.9	_____

Gold _____ **Silver** _____ **Bronze** _____

Judges	1	2	3	4	5	6	7	Final Score
Women								_____
Mary	9.3	9.4	8.9	9.2	8.9	9.0	9.2	_____
Tina	8.9	9.4	8.9	9.0	9.1	9.4	9.3	_____
Chen	9.0	9.0	9.3	8.9	9.2	9.3	9.0	_____
Gail	8.8	9.0	9.1	9.2	8.8	9.2	9.0	_____
Toni	9.2	9.1	8.9	9.2	9.3	8.9	9.0	_____

Gold _____ **Silver** _____ **Bronze** _____

 # Keeping Score

Read the terms related to scoring and name the sport in the box to the right.

1. strike, home run, out, foul _____

2. field goal, free throw, three-point shot _____

3. knockout, decision, disqualification _____

4. form, flips, turns, falls, elements _____

5. love, deuce, advantage, double fault _____

6. throw-in, free kick, offside, penalty kick _____

7. speed, distance, time _____

8. yellow card, side-out, service fault, net ball _____

9. pin, takedown, near fall, escape _____

10. ippon, yuko, hiki wake, waza-aris _____

11. snatch, clean-and-jerk, bench press _____

12. bull's eye, accuracy, distance _____

Word Bank

baseball	gymnastics	track and field
basketball	weightlifting	volleyball
boxing	tennis	judo
wrestling	soccer	archery

Extension: Think of three different sports and write down at least three terms related to each one. Exchange your list with classmates. Can they guess the sports?

What's Your Event?
Gymnastics

Gymnastics is a sport that requires strength, flexibility, and grace. There are four events in a women's gymnastics meet and six events in a men's meet. Some of the events include: balance beam, floor exercise, pommel horse, vault, and still rings. Read these quotes from the parents of five gymnasts. Use the clues to decide which athlete competes in each event.

- "When he was little, he said he wanted to be a rodeo rider. His interest actually increased after we moved to Texas."

- "Monkeys were his favorite zoo animal. He liked to watch them swing in the trees. This worried his father who was hoping he'd be President of the United States."

- "She was our good little girl, we taught her to walk the straight and narrow. She was always smiling."

- "Her mother and I always expected she'd grow up to be a dancer. She was so light on her feet sometimes it seemed that she could fly."

- "I remember when I punished her for jumping off her bed, and there was the time she picked the neighbors' flowers. She was always getting into mischief."

	Balance Beam	Floor Exercise	Pommel Horse	Vault	Still Rings
Dallas					
George					
Joy					
Robin					
Daisy					

What's Your Event?
Track and Field

Track and field competitions include many running, jumping, and throwing events. It is a sport that requires strength, coordination, and speed. Read these quotes from the parents of five track and field athletes. Use the clues to decide which athlete competes in each event.

- "His training started when we moved 2.6 miles from his school. I couldn't drive him, so he had to walk. His sister, Jill, usually got up late and had to run."

- "He was the best outfielder on his baseball team. He could throw a ball all the way to home plate. Last year his Little League team went to the finals in Florida."

- "He wasn't good at team sports, but he could sure throw a Frisbee. We hope he grows up to be an inventor."

- "She was never late to school even when she woke up late. She missed walking with her brother, Jack. Everyone was surprised at how fast she could run."

- "Skipping rope wasn't difficult enough for her, she was a high achiever. She always wanted to win at everything she tried."

	Marathon	Discus Throw	Shot Put	Sprint	High Jump
Jack					
Orlando					
Thomas					
Jill					
Victoria					

Scrambled Games

Unscramble the names of each Olympic sport. Then fill it in the puzzle boxes. Use the key letters to help.

1. insnet _____

2. cyglnic _____

3. chrraey _____

4. tsoflalb _____

5. linigsa_____

6. scocer _____

7. cgniefn _____

8. ahltetisc _____

9. gmynsatisc _____

10. wingor _____

11. llabbsae _____

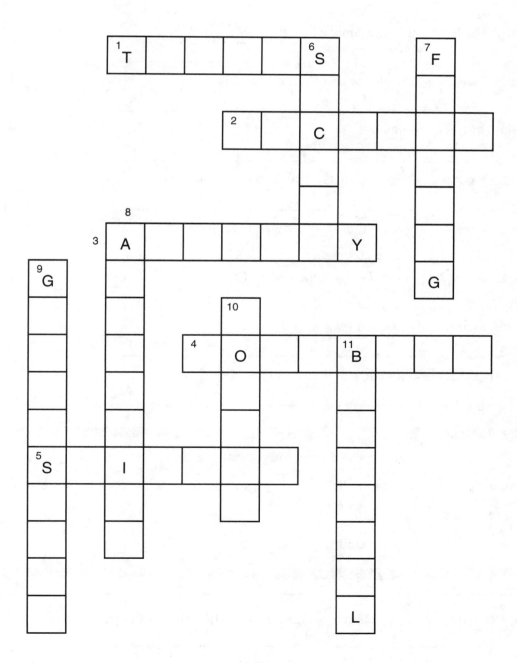

33

Action Words

Read these sentences. Underline the number of verbs indicated by the number. Name the sport.

1. The martial arts athlete uses his hands, feet, knees, elbows, and head to strike an opponent. (2)
   - Sport: _____

2. They enjoy this swim-bike-run race. (1)
   - Sport: _____

3. The heavyweight pins his opponent to the mat. (1)
   - Sport: _____

4. Her vault helps the women's team win the gold medal. (2)
   - Sport: _____

5. The star player hit three home runs. (1)
   - Sport: _____

6. Competitors wear padded gloves and fight in a ring. (2)
   - Sport: _____

7. She jumps off the springboard. (1)
   - Sport: _____

8. In dressage, the rider wears a formal jacket and a top hat. (1)
   - Sport: _____

9. In this sport, the sweeper and the stopper defend the goal. (1)
   - Sport: _____

10. If a player serves two faults, he loses the point. (2)
    - Sport: _____

11. The strong man lifts the barbell over his head. (1)
    - Sport: _____

12. The peloton rides close together in a race. (1)
    - Sport: _____

Word Bank

taekwondo	baseball	diving	equestrian
triathlon	gymnastics	soccer	tennis
wrestling	weightlifting	boxing	cycling

Extension: Rewrite each of the sentences above using the verbs in the past tense.

Olympic Word Pairs

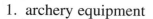 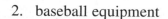

Read the clues and fill in the word pairs. Notice each word pair shares one letter.

1. archery equipment

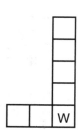

2. baseball equipment

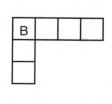

3. soccer positions

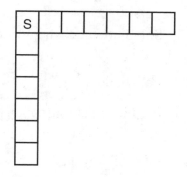

4. boxing time and place

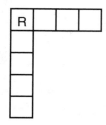

5. cycling races

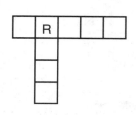

6. equestrian uniform

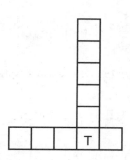

7. dive positions

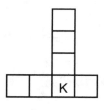

8. originally ping-pong

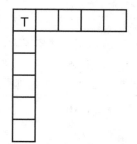

9. net game location

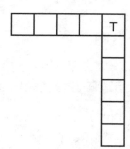

10. short distance events

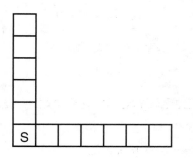

11. track and field throws

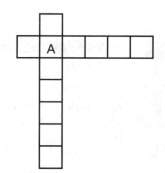

12. footwear

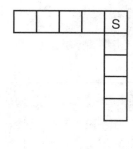

⚜ Definition of Terms ⚜

Use the Word Bank or a dictionary to help identify these sports terms.

1. The score sheet used by a judge in a boxing match:_____

2. Small, toothed wheel located on the rear wheel of a bicycle:_____

3. Group of riders who ride close together in a race: _____

4. Dive position with the legs straight and the body bent at the waist:_____

5. Leaving the apparatus at the end of a gymnastics routine: _____

6. A piece of gymnastic equipment: _____

7. A sword with a curved hand guard that protects the back of the hand: _____

8. The place where baseball pitchers warm up:_____

9. A hit where the player reaches second base safely: _____

10. To slam the ball into the basket from above the rim: _____

11. The length of a pool from one end to the other: _____

12. The stick that is passed in a relay race:_____

Word Bank

card	apparatus	dunk
gear	bullpen	dismount
peloton	pike	saber
baton	double	lap

Extension: Write five sentences using words from the Word Bank. Leave a blank where that word would be. Exchange papers with a classmate. Was your sentence clear enough so that he/she could fill in the blank correctly?

Olympic Firsts

The first Olympic Games were held in Greece more than two thousand years ago. When the Modern Games were revived in 1896, founder Pierre de Coubertin again chose Athens as the host city. In 2004, the Games will return to their birthplace for a third time. Here are some important "firsts" that have changed the Olympic experience. Read the information and decide what year each one occurred. Use the Host Cities list (p. 11) to help you.

First Time Events	Site	Year
1. The Olympic flame was lit.	Amsterdam	_____
2. The Olympic flag was flown. Athletes took the Olympic oath.	Antwerp	_____
3. Women competed in swimming and diving.	Stockholm	_____
4. Taekwondo and triathlon were included as Olympic sports.	Sydney	_____
5. Women competed in canoeing. The Games were televised.	London	_____
6. The torch relay was run.	Berlin	_____
7. The Olympic motto was used.	Paris	_____
8. Judo and volleyball were included as Olympic sports.	Tokyo	_____
9. Men lived in the Olympic Village.	Los Angeles	_____
10. Women competed in basketball.	Montreal	_____
11. Men's basketball was opened to professional players.	Barcelona	_____

Olympic Analogies

An **analogy** is used to compare two ideas. To solve an analogy, determine how the first set of words is related. The next set of words should relate in the same way. Analogies are read as follows:

sink : swim :: hit : _____

"sink" is to "swim" as "hit" is to "_____"

Note that <u>sink</u> and <u>swim</u> are opposites. The correct answer would be the opposite of <u>hit</u>. So,

sink : swim :: hit : miss

Fill in the blanks below to complete the analogies.

1. bow and arrow : archery :: _____ : baseball

2. bicycle : cycling :: _____ : equestrian

3. kicking : soccer :: _____ : tennis

4. boxing : ring :: _____ : court

5. runner : track :: _____ : mat

6. volleyball : hands :: _____ : racket

7. racket : tennis :: _____ : table tennis

8. foil : fencing :: _____ : boxing

9. goal : soccer :: _____ : baseball

10. shoot : arrow :: _____ : javelin

11. inning : baseball :: _____ : boxing

12. pentathlon : five :: _____ : ten

13. tennis : ball :: _____ : birdie or shuttlecock

14. bathing suit : swimming :: _____ : wrestling

15. sprint : short :: _____ : long

Extension: Write three new Olympic analogies.

Venues

There are three main locations for the 2004 Olympic Games: **Athens Olympic Sports Complex, Hellinikon Olympic Complex, and the Faliron Olympic Coastal Zone Complex.** Each complex has more than one field or stadium where athletes practice and compete. They are all located within thirty minutes travel time of the Olympic Village.

- The Athens Olympic Sports Complex is 6.8 miles (11 km) south of the Olympic Village. It houses the Olympic Stadium and will be the venue for six sports: athletics (track and field), basketball, cycling (track), gymnastics, swimming, and tennis.

- The Hellinikon Olympic Complex is 20 miles (32 km) south of the Olympic Village. It will be the venue for five sports: badminton, baseball, softball, fencing, and hockey.

- The Faliron Olympic Coastal Zone Complex is 15 miles (24 km) southwest of the Olympic Village. It contains the Peace and Friendship Indoor Stadium and will be the venue for seven sports: basketball, beach volleyball, volleyball, boxing, handball, judo, and taekwondo.

Create icons for the map legend and then add your icons to the appropriate place on the map.

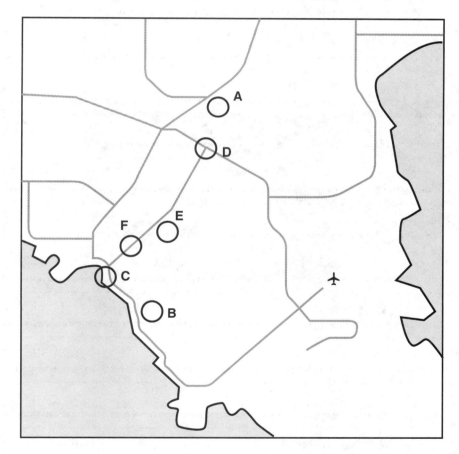

Legend

A	◯	Athens Olympic Sports Complex	D	◯	Athens City Center
B	◯	Hellinikon Olympic Complex	E	◯	Olympic Village
C	◯	Faliron Olympic Coastal Zone Complex	F	◯	Panathinaikon Stadium

Panathinaikon Stadium

The Panathinaikon Stadium was built to host the first modern Olympic Games in 1896.

When the government ran short of funds, a wealthy Greek businessman, George Averoff, donated enough money to have the stadium built so the games could take place on time. There is a statue honoring Averoff in front of the stadium.

The white marble stadium can seat as many as 80,000 spectators. From the top of the horseshoe shaped seating area there is a view of the National Garden and the Acropolis. The stadium is used throughout the year for major sporting events and concerts.

Panathinaikon Stadium has been carefully restored and updated for the 2004 Olympic Games. It has new lighting and fire prevention systems. The track has been redesigned. Athens' historic stadium is ready to host the opening and closing ceremonies, archery events, and the finish of the women's and men's marathons.

Choose one assignment to complete.

- Think of a large sports stadium you have visited. Write a news article explaining five ways it might be improved.
- Research how funds are raised to build new athletic stadiums in cities around the U.S. Share what you learn with the class.
- Old stadiums are usually torn down in the United States. Do research to find information about the oldest professional or college stadium currently being used in your state. Explain its history to the class.
- Compare and contrast two athletic fields or stadiums that you know well. Explain how they are used, what is good/bad about them, and how they might be improved.

 # Pictograms

Use these pictograms in one or more of the following ways:

- Bulletin board displays
- Concentration–style memory games (Match a pictogram with a word card.)
- Creating board games
- Illustrating original books or sports encyclopedias
- Make an Olympic quilt. Enlarge the squares and glue them onto tagboard. Simulate "stitching" around each piece with a crayon or marker.
- Mobiles to hang from your ceiling
- Charades or Twenty Questions
- Sequencing in alphabetical order
- Categorizing by various attributes (ball/no ball, speed/strength, outdoors/indoors, etc.)
- Story starters

Archery

Athletics

Badminton

Baseball

Pictograms *(cont.)*

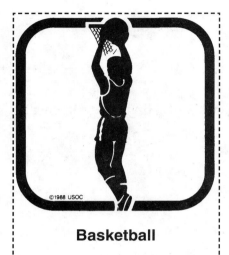

Basketball

Boxing

Canoeing/Kayaking

Cycling

Diving

Fencing

Gymnastics

Equestrian

Field Hockey

Judo

Modern Pentathlon

Rowing

Sailing

Shooting

Soccer

Softball

Swimming

Synchronized Swimming

Table Tennis

Taekwondo

Tennis

Team Handball

Triathlon

Volleyball

Weightlifting

Water Polo

Wrestling

 # The Marathon

The 2004 Athens Olympic marathon will travel the original route of Pheidippides, a strong Greek runner, who ran from the Plain of Marathon to Athens in 490 B.C. to announce the victory of the Greeks over the invading Persian army. Legend says that he delivered a one word message, "Nenikekamen" ("We won.") before he collapsed and died.

Spyridon Louis, a 25-year old Greek shepherd, won the 1896 marathon, finishing seven minutes ahead of the next closest runner. He was joined in a victory lap by the Royal Princes of Greece. Louis became a national hero after his victory.

Choose one of these famous Olympic marathon runners. Do research to learn more about their lives and athletic achievements. Fill in the information.

Spyridon Louis, Greece   Waldemar Cierpinski, East Germany

Emil Zatopek, Czechoslovakia   Carlos Lopez, Portugal

Alain Mimoun, France   Joan Benoit, USA

Abebe Bekila, Ethiopia   Rosa Moto, Portugal

Athlete's name: _____   Home Country: _____

Olympic Games year(s): _____   Events won: _____

Records set (if any): _____

Three interesting facts about the athlete:

_____

_____

_____

Write a brief report to share with your class on the back of this paper.

Extension: Use a map to find a location 26 miles from your home. Travel the distance in a car and make a list of the things you see along the way

Design an "Athlon"

"Athlon" is a Greek word meaning *contest*. Several Olympic events include more than one contest. In the *triathlon*, meaning three contests, the competitor must run, swim, and cycle. Other Summer Olympic multi-contest events include the modern *pentathlon*, *heptathlon,* and the *decathlon*.

Think about your favorites sports and games. Use these Greek prefixes to help you name and create your own "athlon".

di = **2**   tri = **3**   tetra = **4**   penta = **5**   hexa = **6**

hepta = **7**   octo = **8**   ennea = **9**   deca = **10**

Name your event: _____

List the contests: _____

_____

What equipment would the competitors need? _____

_____

What type of clothing or uniform would be best? _____

_____

Where would these contests be held? _____

_____

What physical characteristics would make a good competitor for this event? _____

_____

_____

 # Medal Winners

Update the chart below each morning with information from the previous day's Olympic events. Report the athlete's name, country, sport, and medal of all winners and enter them on the list. You can find the information on the Internet or in a daily newspaper.

Sport	Athlete's Name	Country	Gold	Silver	Bronze

Bonus: Organize your information in a different way on the back of this paper.

- Make a graph showing the totals for each kind of medal (gold, silver, bronze).
- Make a graph showing the total medals for each sport.
- Make a graph showing the total medals for each country.

 # Newsmakers

To answer the questions in the blank below, read this sentence from a newspaper article about a famous Olympian:

"Rulon Gardner made a comeback within his reach Sunday in Indianapolis, earning a shot at the world gold medal in heavyweight Greco-Roman wrestling."

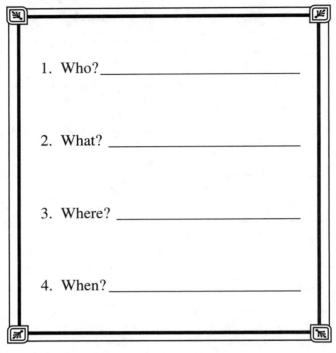

1. Who?_____

2. What? _____

3. Where? _____

4. When? _____

Find two news articles about Olympic athletes. Glue each one to a separate sheet of colored paper. Cut out the boxes below and glue one on each sheet of paper, alongside the article. Then, answer the questions about each article.

1. Who?_____

2. What? _____

3. Where? _____

4. When? _____

1. Who?_____

2. What? _____

3. Where? _____

4. When? _____

☙🏛 Television Reporter 🏛☙

Complete this form after watching one Olympic event.

Sport:_____

Time: _____

Location: _____

Who competed? _____

_____

Describe the uniforms: _____

_____

Describe the venue:_____

_____

Explain the rules: _____

_____

Who were the medal winners?

Gold _____ _____
            (name)   (country)

Silver _____ _____
            (name)   (country)

Bronze _____ _____
            (name)   (country)

Describe the medal ceremony: _____

_____

On the back of this paper, draw a picture of an athlete competing in this sport.

Extension: Would you have preferred to have seen this event live, in the stadium, or was it better to have seen it on television? Why?

 # Postcard Home

Pretend you are one of the athletes mentioned on the "Newsmakers" or "Television Reporter" pages. Write a postcard to your family or friends telling about your Olympic experience. Be sure to include some details about your competition. Then cut out the postcard and add a picture that illustrates what you've written.

Measuring Up

Below are playing courts for three popular Olympic sports: basketball, tennis, and volleyball. Use these dimensions to find the perimeter and area of each playing court.

To find the **perimeter** (distance around), add all four sides together.

To find the **area**, multiply one short side by one long side.

Do all your calculations on another sheet of paper.

Volleyball Court	Tennis Court	Basketball Court
P = _____	P = _____	P = _____
A = _____	A = _____	A = _____

Basketball Court

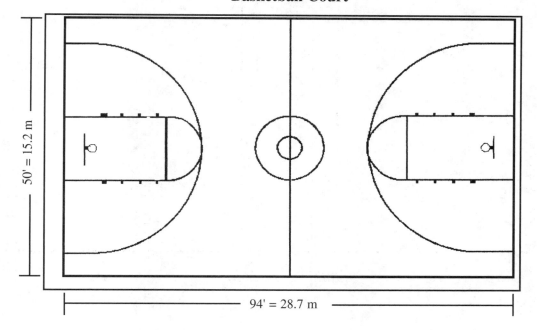

50' = 15.2 m

94' = 28.7 m

Tennis Court

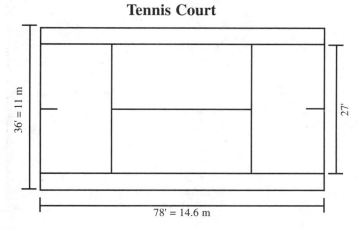

36' = 11 m

27'

78' = 14.6 m

Volleyball Court

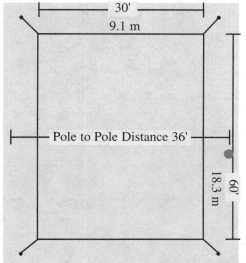

30'

9.1 m

Pole to Pole Distance 36'

60'

18.3 m

 # Making a Mascot

The Olympic Games mascot always represents the host city and country in some way. Phèvos and Athenà, the official mascots for the Athens 2004 Olympic Games, are designed to look like ancient Greek dolls. The brother and sister take their names from Greek mythology. Athenà was the Goddess of Wisdom and the protector of the city of Athens. Phèvos Apollo was the God of Light and Music. Phèvos and Athenà represent Greece and the Olympic values of cooperation, fair play, friendship, and equality.

Think about the city in which you live or a city that you know well. What makes it special? Draw a mascot for the city you have chosen. On the lines below, explain your design and what it represents.

 # The Olympic Flag

Baron de Coubertin, the founder of the modern Olympic Games, designed the Olympic flag. He used five rings to stand for the continents of the world, North and South America (counted as one), Europe, Asia, Africa, and Australia. The rings are blue, yellow, black, green, and red because at least one of those colors is on every flag in the world. The rings are in the center of a plain white background. They are interlocking to represent the friendship and cooperation of athletes around the world.

The Olympic Committee adopted the flag in 1914, and it was first flown at the 1920 Antwerp Games. Eight people carry the flag into the stadium for the opening ceremony. Five of the flag bearers represent the different continents and three stand for the Olympic ideals of sport, environment, and culture.

Work with three of your friends to design a flag that represents the interests, values, beliefs, and diversity of the members of your class. Draw your flag in the space below. Share your design with the class. Be ready to explain what each symbol and color represents.

Medals

No medals were awarded in the ancient Olympic Games. First place winners were given a wreath made from an olive branch to wear on their heads. Second and third place winners got nothing. In the 1896 Olympic Games, first place winners received silver medals. The first gold medals were awarded eight years later at the 1904 Olympic Games in St. Louis.

Olympic medals are almost three inches (seven cm) in diameter. Since 1928, they have had a Greek goddess, the Olympic Rings, the stadium of ancient Athens, a Greek vase, and a horse drawn chariot on the front. Also included are the Olympiad number, year, and name of the host city. Host cities may add more details to the front and can design the back of the medals as they wish.

Look at the Olympic medal design below. Add the following to the medal: "Olympiad XXVIII", "Athens", "2004", and the Olympic rings.

Choose one to complete:

1. Use the search terms "Olympic medal winners" to find a list of medal winners from previous Olympic Games on the Internet. Print your findings to share with the class.

2. Make a poster or diorama showing an ancient or a modern medal ceremony.

3. Write a brief news article about a recent Olympic medal winner. Include information about his/her sport, achievement, and records, if any.

Torch Relay

The Olympic flame is one of the most important symbols of the Games. It was first used at the 1936 Berlin Olympic Games. Since then, lighting the flame has been an important part of every opening ceremony. The idea of keeping a flame lit during the Games was first used by the ancient Greeks at Olympia.

The torch for the Athens 2004 is made of aluminum and wood from the olive tree. It is 27 inches (68 cm) long and weighs 25 oz. (700 grams). It will be carried by 10,000 torchbearers from around the world, traveling for 35 days and visiting 27 cities before it returns to Greece.

The torch will be lit by the sun's rays in Olympia, Greece, in May, 2004. The torch relay will begin in Sydney, Australia, and continue to every continent, including South America and Africa for the first time. It will call on the people of the world to celebrate the Olympic values of athleticism, peace, and friendship.

The torch relay will include every city that has ever hosted the Olympic Games, plus the host city for the 2008 Olympic Games, Beijing, China. Six other cities were approved for the torch relay by the International Olympic Committee. They are: Cairo, Egypt; Cape Town, South Africa; Rio De Janeiro, Brazil; New York City, USA; Lausanne, Switzerland; and Nicosia, Cyprus.

Since the modern Olympic Games began in 1896, these cities have hosted them:

Athens, Greece

Paris, France

St. Louis, Missouri (USA)

London, England

Stockholm, Sweden

Berlin, Germany

Antwerp, Belgium

Amsterdam, The Netherlands

Los Angeles, California (USA)

Helsinki, Finland

Melbourne, Australia

Rome, Italy

Tokyo, Japan

Mexico City, Mexico

Munich, Germany

Montreal, Canada

Moscow, Russia

Seoul, South Korea

Barcelona, Spain

Atlanta, Georgia (USA)

Choose one of these activities:

1. Use the information in this article to trace the route of the Olympic torch relay on the World Map (pages 56–57). You should begin at Sydney, Australia, and end at Athens, Greece.

2. Make a list showing at least two Olympians from each Olympic host country.

3. Do research and write a story explaining the characteristics that make these cities good choices for the Olympic Games in summer.

4. Choose one city and do research to explain how the Olympic venues there are being used today. For Internet research, type in the words "Olympic venues" and the name of the city you've chosen. (Example: Olympic venues, Melbourne)

5. Think of at least one reason why each of the six non-host cities might have been chosen by the International Olympic Committee.

World Map

North America

South America

Throwing Simulations

Both the discus and javelin throw were part of the Olympic Games in ancient Greece. In those times, the winner of the discus was considered to be the strongest and best athlete in the world. The hammer throw and shot put probably began in Ireland or Scotland.

To try these sports, you will need:

> softball (shot put)
>
> Frisbee (discus)
>
> lemon in a tube sock (hammer throw)
>
> broom stick or yard stick (javelin)

Preparations: Use chalk to draw a circle (seven feet in diameter) on the playground. For the javelin simulation, designate a running path (about 20 feet long).

For sequenced photos of each throw, access this site: *http://www.advantageathletics.com/*

Please note: To assure the safety of all participants, these activities should be done with adult supervision.

Follow these instructions to simulate each throw.

1. **Shot put**—Throwers should hold the softball in one hand and press it under the chin. They will bend over at the waist and rock or bounce on one leg toward the front of the circle. Then they turn the body and push, or "put," the ball as far as possible. The ball may not drop below shoulder level during the throw.

2. **Discus**—Throwers should hold the Frisbee flat in one hand and release it with a sidearm motion. The Frisbee should spin as it floats through the air.

3. **Hammer Throw**—Throwers should begin by swinging the weighted sock through the air in an arc so that it passes above the head and below the knees. Then, they will spin around several times before releasing the sock.

4. **Javelin**—Please note—Javelin throwers should wear spiked shoes because they will do some running. They will hold the broomstick in one hand and sprint down a path to a foul line. Before reaching the foul line, they will turn, and pull back the arm holding the stick. They will let the stick fly just as they reach the line.

Discuss:

Why are these throwing methods the most efficient for distance and accuracy?

Extension:

Suggest and test other throwing methods and compare the results.

Science Enrichment

Bouncing

Balls are necessary equipment for the Olympic sports of baseball, basketball, soccer, softball, team handball, tennis, and vollyball. They are designed for a specific sport based on their size, weight, and elasticity. This experiment will help you understand that balls will react differently when bounced on a variety of surfaces.

You will need:

- any or all: basketball, baseball, soccer ball, volleyball, tennis ball
- yardstick
- access to any or all of these surfaces: carpet, grass, tile, concrete, wood

Directions:

1. Predict which ball will bounce the highest when dropped from a specific height. Record your predictions on a sheet of paper. Drop the balls and record the results. Compare your predictions with the final outcome.

2. Predict the number of times each ball will bounce when dropped from a specific height. Record your predictions on a sheet of paper. Drop the balls and record the number of bounces. Compare your predictions with the number of actual bounces.

3. Repeat for all surfaces. Create charts to show your results in two ways: Type of ball and type of surface.

Floating

The ability to float is necessary in the Olympic sports of sailing and swimming. Whether an object sinks or floats in water depends on its density and buoyancy. You will draw conclusions about the physical properties of several different objects and use the information to describe and categorize the objects.

You will need:

- large plastic container, half full of water
- 6 to 10 different items including: plastic bottles, toy wood block, paper tubes, bathtub toy, blackboard eraser, rubber ball, ball of clay, plastic or metal bottle caps, foam meat tray, sponge, apple, empty or full milk carton

Directions:

1. Predict if each items will sink or float. Record your prediction on a sheet of paper.
2. Compare your predictions with the actual results.
3. Draw conclusions about the physical properties of the items.

 # Art Project

Students may make a T-shirt or vest from cut paper to display their original Olympic designs. Use the finished items for a bulletin board titled, "Official Olympic Merchandise". You may extend this project with designs for caps, shoes, socks, umbrellas, and jewelry.

Enlarge the diagrams below to 4½" x 6" (11.4 cm x 15.2 cm) and cut several of each from tagboard. Make them available at a center for use by individuals or small groups.

Students will need:

- scissors
- 9" x 12" (22.9 cm x 30.5 cm) construction paper
- pencil, markers

Directions:

1. Fold the construction paper in half along the 12" (30.5 cm) side.
2. Choose a pattern and place the straight side on the fold.
3. Trace around all sides.
4. Cut on the lines.
5. Use markers to decorate the T-shirt or vest with Olympic pins, emblems, or other symbols.

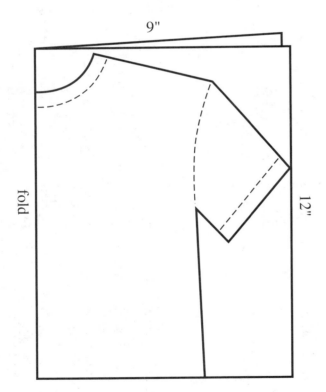 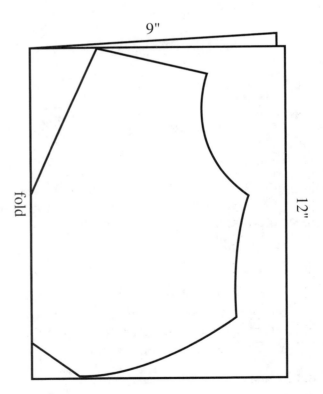

 # Olympic Trivia

Here is some interesting Olympic information to share with your students.

The revival of the modern Olympic Games in 1896 included athletes from 14 countries with the largest groups coming from Greece, Germany, and France.

In 1896, athletes competed in nine sports, divided into 43 events. Today, the Olympic schedule includes 28 sports and 296 events.

The International Olympic Committee (IOC) announced that Athens would host the 2004 Olympic Games on September 5th, 1997.

More than 2,750 volunteers will be needed for the Athens 2004 Olympic Games. In addition to these, 8,000 volunteers will perform in the opening ceremonies.

The 2004 mascots, Athenà and Phèvos, were inspired by ancient Greek dolls called daidala. The original dolls had bell shaped bodies made of terracotta. They wore tunics and had movable legs.

Andreas Varotsos, a native Athenian, was the creator of the 2004 Olympic torch. He studied industrial design in Rome and worked as an industrial designer for some of the biggest companies in Greece.

Coca-Cola is the Olympic Movement's longest standing continuous partner, including every Olympic Games since 1928.

It is expected there will be 50,000 meals served at the Olympic Village every day. Meals will be made using 1,500 international recipes and about 100 tons of food.

Greece's Public Transport Agencies will provide transportation for 600,000 spectators and volunteers each day during the Games.

The International Olympic Committee (IOC) controls all licensing, manufacture, and distribution of the five-ring symbol, emblem, and official mascot. Only companies approved by the IOC may display or use those images on their merchandise.

Greece has a long tradition of excellence in weightlifting. These Greek lifters have won Olympic medals: Alexandros Nikolopoulos, bronze (1896), Sotiris Versis, bronze (1896), Periklis Kakousis, gold (1904), Pyrros Dimas, gold (1992, 1996, 2000), Khaki Kahniashvili, gold (1996, 2000), Valerios Leonidis, silver (1996), Leonidas Sabanis, silver (1996, 2000), Leonidas Kokkas, silver (1996), Viktor Mitrou, silver (2000), and Ioanna Hatziioannou, bronze (2000).

 # Answer Key

Page 22: Olympic Oath

Be a good sport and play fair.

Page 29: Diving

Men:

Tom: 75.77

Bob: 76.61 (Gold)

Joe: 76.44 (Silver)

Paul: 75.94

Tony: 76.10 (Bronze)

Women:

Mary: 76.61 (Silver)

Tina: 76.78 (Gold)

Chen: 76.44 (Bronze)

Gail: 75.77

Toni: 76.27

Page 30: Keeping Score

1. baseball
2. basketball
3. boxing
4. gymnastics
5. tennis
6. soccer
7. track and field
8. volleyball
9. wrestling
10. judo
11. weightlifting
12. archery

Page 31: What's Your Event?
(Gymnastics)

Dallas—pommel horse

George—still rings

Joy—balance beam

Robin—floor exercise

Daisy—vault

Page 32: What's Your Event?
(Track and Field)

Jack—marathon

Orlando—shot put

Thomas—discus throw

Jill—sprint

Victoria—high jump

Page 33: Scrambled Games

1. tennis
2. cycling
3. archery
4. softball
5. sailing
6. soccer
7. fencing
8. athletics
9. gymnastics
10. rowing
11. baseball

Page 34: Action Words

1. uses, strike—taekwondo
2. enjoy—triathlon
3. pins—wrestling
4. helps, win—gymnastics
5. hit—baseball
6. wear, fight—boxing
7. jumps—diving
8. wears—equestrian
9. defend—soccer
10. serves, loses—tennis
11. lifts—weightlifting
12. rides—cycling

Answer Key

Page 35: Olympic Word Pairs

1. arrow, bow
2. bat, ball
3. sweeper, striker
4. round, ring
5. track, road
6. helmet, boots
7. tuck, pike
8. table, tennis
9. tennis, court
10. relays, sprints
11. hammer, javelin
12. shoes, socks

Page 36: Definition of Terms

1. card
2. gear
3. peloton
4. pike
5. dismount
6. apparatus
7. saber
8. bullpen
9. double
10. dunk
11. lap
12. baton

Page 37: Olympic Firsts

1. 1928
2. 1920
3. 1912
4. 2000
5. 1948
6. 1936
7. 1924
8. 1964
9. 1932
10. 1976
11. 1992

Page 38: Olympic Analogies

1. ball and bat
2. horse
3. hitting
4. tennis
5. wrestler
6. tennis
7. paddle
8. glove
9. home run
10. throw
11. round
12. decathlon
13. badminton
14. singlet
15. marathon

Page 51: Court Side Measurement—

Basketball:
    P = 288 ft. (87.8 m)
    A = 4700 sq. ft. (436.6 sq. m)

Tennis:
    P = 228 ft. (69.5 m)
    A = 2808 sq. ft. (260.9 sq. m.)

Volleyball:
    P = 180 ft. (54.9 m)
    A = 1800 sq. ft. (167.2 sq. m)

 # Bibliography

Anderson, Dave. *The Story of the Olympics*. HarperCollins Juvenile Books, 2000.

Arnold, Caroline. *The Summer Olympics*. Franklin Watts, Inc., 1991.

Bauer, Larry. *Easy Olympic Sports Readers*. Teacher Created Materials, Inc., 1998.

Fischer, David. *The Encyclopedia of the Summer Olympics*. Franklin Watts Inc., 2003.

Hennessey, B. G. *Olympics!* Puffin Books, 2000.

Holzschuher, Cynthia. *United States Olympic Committee's Curriculum Guide to the Olympic Games: The Olympic Dream*. Griffin Publishing/Teacher Created Materials, Inc., 2000.

Knotts, Bob. *The Summer Olympics (True Books - Sports)*. Children's Book Press, 2000.

Kristy, Davida. *Coubertin's Olympics: How the Games Began*. Lerner Publishing, 2003.

Ledeboer, Suzanne. *Olympism: A Basic Guide to the History, Ideals, and Sports of the Olympic Movement*. Griffin Publishing, 2001.

Middleton, Hayden. *Great Olympic Moments*. Heinemann Library, 1999.

Osbourne, Mary Pope. *Hour of the Olympics*. Random House, 1998.

Oxlade, Chris. *Eyewitness: Olympics*. DK Publishing, 2000.

Ross, Stewart. *The Original Olympics*. Peter Bendrick Books, 1999.

Web Sites

http://www.athens2004.com

http://www.forthnet.gr/olympics/athens1896/

http://www.olympic.org

http://www.greece-2004.com/athens_2004_olympic_games/

http://www.olympiceducation.gr/intro/intro.asp

http://www.sikids.com

http://www.timeforkids.com

http://www.worldalmanacforkids.com/explore/sports/olympics.html